The Raven and the Fox

PICTURE WINDOW BOOKS
a capstone imprint

First published in the United States in 2011
by Picture Window Books
A Capstone Imprint
151 Good Counsel Drive
P.O. Box 669
Mankato, Minnesota 56002
www.capstonepub.com

Library of Congress Cataloging-in-Publication data is available on the Library of Congress website.
ISBN 978-1-4048-6502-0 (library binding)

Summary: A sly fox outwits a prideful raven in this retelling of Aesop's classic fable.

Art Director: Kay Fraser
Graphic Designer: Emily Harris
Production Specialist: Michelle Biedscheid

Printed in the United States of America in North Mankato, Minnesota.
092010

005933CGS11

The Raven and the Fox

retold by Roberto Piumini

illustrated by Raffaella Bolaffio

Once upon a time, there was a large raven with soot-black feathers and a gray beak. One day, he was flying around in search of something to eat. As he flew, he carefully studied the countryside below.

Every now and then, a rush of air carried the raven up, higher and higher. From there, the raven could see all across the land.

Along the edge of the forest, a red fox with a long, fluffy tail was also searching for food. The fox sniffed at the ground. His ears twitched, ready to catch the slightest sound.

Seeing the shadow of the raven flying above him, the fox lifted his head. He watched the raven soar, almost in envy.

Suddenly the delicious aroma of cheese drifted over from a nearby field. The fox turned toward the smell and saw a peasant man sound asleep under a tree, with his hat over his eyes.

On a nearby rock, a napkin was carefully spread out. A lovely piece of cheese sat on top of it.

The fox carefully crept forward. Human beings could be dangerous, but the smell of that cheese was irresistible. The fox was almost drooling with anticipation.

With just a few steps to go, the fox stopped to watch the man's feet. This was always a good way to tell whether a human was sleeping or just pretending. The feet were completely still. The man was truly asleep.

Just as the fox was about to jump forward, a shadow passed swiftly on the ground in front of him. The raven flew down to the piece of cloth. Without even folding his wings, he opened his beak, plucked up the cheese, and flew off.

The fox watched, motionless. Only his nose followed the flight of the raven. When he saw the raven fly into the forest, he darted away in that direction.

The raven perched on a high branch to get into a comfortable position so he could eat his cheese. Meanwhile, the fox slowly walked into the woods, looking like he didn't have a care in the world. Then he lifted his nose and spoke, "Oh, look! It's the raven! Just my luck!"

The raven peered down over the piece of cheese.

The fox sat and gazed up at the raven. His tail swept the grass lazily.

"You know, Raven," said the fox, "I've always asked myself why you aren't the one to be called bird of paradise, instead of that feathery creature with the soft tail."

Now curious, the raven tilted his head.

The fox continued, "I'm not talking about flying. There are other birds who can fly like you. No, I'm talking about your feathers, ten times blacker and shinier than the blackest rabbit. And then there's your beak. It's like a gray pearl!"

The raven took a small step sideways. He was about to lay down the piece of cheese so he could thank the fox, but there was no room.

Suddenly, the fox brought his tail straight up into the air.
"Now I understand why you're not called bird of paradise!"
he shouted.

The raven took another step sideways, waiting. The fox's tail
went back to moving lazily over the grass.

"The fact is that you have no voice," said the fox. "That must
be the reason."

The raven flapped his wings nervously. *What?* he thought. *No voice? Nonsense!*

The raven opened his beak wide, and a great "CAW" echoed throughout the forest. He even woke the man sleeping in the field.

And the piece of cheese fell straight down, like a rock, right in front of the fox.

The fox grinned. "Ah, wait!" he declared, putting out a paw to hold down the cheese. "That's not the reason, either. You've got a voice. What you're missing is a brain!"

And with that, the fox picked up the cheese and trotted off to his den.

The raven sat there for a moment, his beak still wide open with surprise. Finally, the raven shut his beak, and all he was left with was the sour taste of having been tricked.

Fairy Tale Follow-Up

1. At the beginning of the story, the fox watches the raven soar overhead, almost in envy. Why was the fox envious of the raven?

2. Do you think a fox would really eat a chunk of cheese? What about a raven? What other foods could have been used?

3. The story says the fox drooled with anticipation. He really hoped to eat the cheese, but then the raven swiped it away. How do you think the fox felt after that happened?

4. Did you guess what the fox was trying to do when he began talking to the raven?

5. *The Raven and the Fox* is a type of story called a fable. Fables normally teach a lesson. What lesson does this fable teach?

ᴏ⊙ Glossary ⊙ᴏ

anticipation (an-tiss-uh-PAY-shun)—the expectation that something will happen and the preparation for it to happen

aroma (uh-ROH-muh)—a smell that is usually pleasant

bird of paradise (BURD UHV PA-ruh-dise)—a type of bird known for its bright, fluffy feathers

irresistible (ihr-uh-ZISS-tuh-buhl)—too tempting to resist

perched (PURCHD)—sat or stood on the edge of something, often high up

twitched (TWICHD)—made small jerky movements

Fun Facts about Ravens & Foxes

It is no wonder than many stories, like *The Raven and the Fox*, feature animals as characters. They are clever, curious, and sometimes funny. Here are a few facts that show how fascinating the raven and the fox are in real life.

Ravens eat fruits, seeds, nuts, fish, small animals, food remains, and even garbage. They sometimes steal food from other animals.

Foxes are not picky eaters at all! They eat a variety of food — from squirrels to plants to eggs.

The raven is the topic — and title — of a very famous poem by Edgar Allan Poe.

Kitsune is a foxlike figure in Japanese folklore. This powerful animal spirit is known for being tricky and cunning.

Ravens can express happiness, surprise, anger, and other emotions with their call.

Red foxes often live in abandoned wolf dens or large squirrel burrows.

Ravens are extremely good fliers. They use skills to chase, dive, and roll when trying to attract mates.

Foxes are members of the dog family, but they have many catlike characteristics. They are good climbers and play with their food before eating it, just like cats.

Experts believe that ravens mate for life. Females lay three to seven eggs at a time, and after they hatch, both parents care for the young.

Ravens live an average of thirteen years in the wild.

In the wild, foxes live two to five years. In captivity, they have been known to live up to twelve to fourteen years.

About the Author

Roberto Piumini lives and works in his native Italy. He has worked with children as both a teacher and a theater actor/entertainer. He credits these experiences for inspiring the youthful language of his many books. With his crisp and imaginative way of dealing with every kind of subject, Roberto charms his young readers. His award-winning books, for both children and adults, have been translated into many languages.

About the Illustrator

Raffaella Bolaffio is an illustrator in her native country of Italy. She specializes in writing and illustrating books for children.